First Facts™

Simple Machines to the Rescue

Pulleys to the Rescue

by Sharon Thales

Consultant:
Louis A. Bloomfield, PhD
Professor of Physics
University of Virginia
Charlottesville, Virginia

Capstone press®

Mankato, Minnesota

First Facts is published by Capstone Press,
151 Good Counsel Drive, P.O. Box 669, Mankato, Minnesota 56002.
www.capstonepress.com

Library of Congress Cataloging-in-Publication Data
Thales, Sharon.
    Pulleys to the rescue / Sharon Thales.
    p. cm.—(First facts. Simple machines to the rescue)
    Summary: "Describes pulleys, including what they are, how they work, past uses, and
common uses of these simple machines today"—Provided by publisher.
    Includes bibliographical references and index.
    ISBN-13: 978-0-7368-6748-1 (hardcover)
    ISBN-10: 0-7368-6748-1 (hardcover)
    1. Pulleys—Juvenile literature. I. Title. II. Series.
TJ1103.T47 2007
621.8—dc22   2006021503

Editorial Credits
Becky Viaene, editor; Thomas Emery, designer; Kyle Grenz, illustrator; Jo Miller,
    photo researcher/photo editor

Photo Credits
Art Directors/Constance Toms, 6
Capstone Press/Karon Dubke, 10, 14, 21 (all); TJ Thoraldson Digital Photography, cover
Getty Images Inc./AFP/Sajjad Hussain, 5
Mary Evans Picture Library, 9
Peter Arnold/Bilderberg/Dorothea Schmid, 15
PhotoEdit Inc./Dennis MacDonald, 18
Shutterstock/Christian Lagerek, 12–13; Igor Karon, 17

1 2 3 4 5 6 12 11 10 09 08 07

Table of Contents

A Helpful Pulley

Your mom's car won't start. How can she move her heavy car to a repair shop?

Pulley to the rescue!

Your mom can call a tow truck. A tow truck has a large hook connected to a **pulley**. The pulley makes it easier to lift the car and move it.

4

Pulley

Pulley

Work It

A pulley is a **simple machine**. Simple machines have one or no moving parts. Machines are used to make **work** easier.

Work is using a **force** to move an object. Pulleys usually help people do work by moving heavy objects.

Pulley Fact

Not sure what a pulley looks like? A pulley is a wheel with a groove around the edge. A rope, belt, or chain in the groove turns the wheel.

A Pulley in Time

In ancient Greece, hundreds of men worked to move a newly built ship into the water. They needed an easier way to move heavy ships.

Pulleys to the rescue!

A scientist named Archimedes arranged ropes and pulley wheels so one person could do the job. The ropes were longer, so the force traveled farther, but less force was needed.

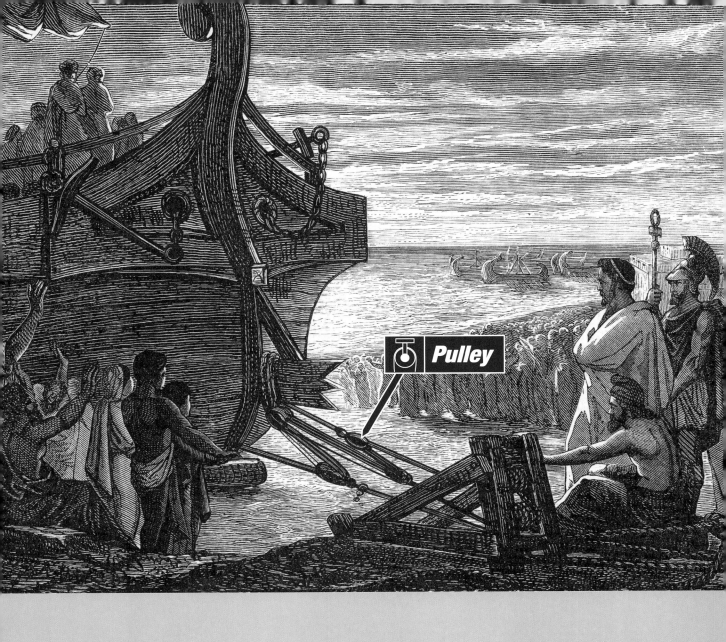

Pulley

Fixed Pulleys

Fixed pulleys help you lift objects that weigh less than you. A fixed pulley is joined to something, such as a flagpole.

When you use a fixed pulley, the direction of force changes. Pull down on the rope and the flag goes up. The pulley wheel turns, but it doesn't move up or down with the flag and rope.

Movable Pulleys

Want to lift a heavy object? Movable pulleys help people lift big cargo boxes and other heavy loads.

Instead of attaching the rope to the load, attach a movable pulley. The rope moves through both sides of the pulley wheel. Each side of the rope supports half of the load's weight. Then, you only have to pull half as hard to lift a heavy load.

Pulley

Pulley Fact

The more pulleys you have working together, the easier it is to lift a heavy load.

What Would We Do Without Pulleys?

At the store, you and your mom put groceries on a **conveyor belt.** Helpful pulleys are hidden under the belt. They help move the items to the cashier.

Pulleys

Pulley

Large pulleys also help skiers and snowboarders. These simple machines help move people on chair lifts along a cable to hilltops.

Working Together

People stand on platforms to wash windows on tall buildings. Platforms are **complex machines**. They are made of several simple machines.

Pulleys lower and raise a platform. Wheels and axles on the platform help it ride smoothly against the building.

Pulley Buddies

Six kinds of simple machines combine to make almost every machine there is.

- **Inclined plane**–a slanting surface that is used to move objects to different levels

- **Lever**–a bar that turns on a resting point and is used to lift items

- **Pulley**–a grooved wheel turned by a rope, belt, or chain that often moves heavy objects

- **Screw**–an inclined plane wrapped around a post that usually holds objects together

- **Wedge**–an inclined plane that moves to split things apart or push them together

- **Wheel and axle**–a wheel that turns around a bar to move objects

Pulley

Pulleys Everywhere

Pulleys help people every day. Cranes have big pulleys that move heavy loads, including boats.

Little pulleys help people move window blinds up and down. Whether it's big or small, pulleys help move it all.

Amazing but True!

In ancient times, Greeks needed to stop Romans from attacking by ship. Pulleys in a machine called the claw of Archimedes came to the rescue.

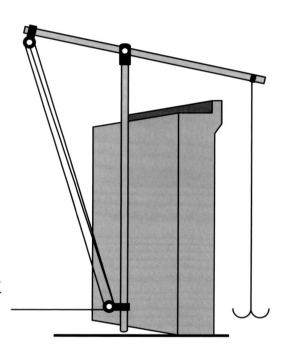

This machine's giant hook grabbed Roman ships that sailed too close to Greek land. Oxen tugged on pulleys connected to the hook to lift the ships. Then Greeks dropped the ships and they smashed into pieces.

Hands On: Working with a Pulley

What You Need

hole punch, paper or plastic cup, 2 long pieces of string, chopstick, empty spool, 10 pennies

What You Do

1. Use the hole punch to make a hole just under the rim of the cup. Make another hole on the opposite side of the cup.

2. Knot one piece of string inside one of the holes. Pull the other end of the string through the other hole and knot it. This makes a handle.

3. Tie one end of the other piece of string to the middle of the string handle.

4. Push the chopstick through the middle of the spool. This is your pulley.

5. In one hand, hold the chopstick. In the other hand, hold the loose end of the long string. Rest the middle of the string across the top of the spool. Place 10 pennies in the cup. Pull on the string.

   You used the pulley to do work. You applied force by pulling on the string. The force lifted the cup filled with pennies.

Glossary

complex machine (KOM-pleks muh-SHEEN)—a machine made of two or more simple machines

conveyor belt (kuhn-VAY-ur BELT)—a belt moved by pulleys that carries items from one area to another

force (FORSS)—a push or a pull

pulley (PUL-ee)—a grooved wheel turned by a rope, belt, or chain that often moves heavy objects

simple machine (SIM-puhl muh-SHEEN)—a tool with one or no moving parts that moves an object when you push or pull; pulleys are simple machines.

work (WURK)—when a force moves an object

Read More

Dahl, Michael. *Pull, Lift, and Lower: A Book about Pulleys.* Amazing Science. Minneapolis: Picture Window Books, 2005.

Oxlade, Chris. *Pulleys.* Useful Machines. Chicago: Heinemann Library, 2003.

Tiner, John Hudson. *Pulleys.* Simple Machines. North Mankato, Minn.: Smart Apple Media, 2003.

Internet Sites

FactHound offers a safe, fun way to find Internet sites related to this book. All of the sites on FactHound have been researched by our staff.

Here's how:

1. Visit *www.facthound.com*

2. Choose your grade level.

3. Type in this book ID **0736867481** for age-appropriate sites. You may also browse subjects by clicking on letters, or by clicking on pictures and words.

4. Click on the **Fetch It** button.

FactHound will fetch the best sites for you!

Index